RABBIT TRICK

by

Alex Hughes

A Mindspace Investigations

Short Story

With bonus short stories

"The Carousel" & "Inky Black Sea"

Alexandra Hughes LLC
4150 Macland Road, Suite 50 #83
Powder Springs, GA 30127
alex@ahugheswriter.com
www.ahugheswriter.com

Publisher's Note: This is a work of fiction. Names, characters, places, and incidents are a product of the author's imagination. Locales and public names are sometimes used for atmospheric purposes. Any resemblance to actual people, living or dead, or to businesses, companies, events, institutions, or locales is completely coincidental.

Book Layout ©2015 BookDesignTemplates.com

Ordering Information:
Quantity sales. Special discounts are available on quantity purchases by corporations, associations, and others. For details, contact the "Special Sales Department" at the address above.

Rabbit Trick/ Alex Hughes. -- 1st ed.
ISBN 978-0-9916429-1-5

Contents

Cherabino called me in the middle of the night, 3 a.m. to be precise.

"I thought we were day shift," I muttered into the phone, my eyes still gummy with sleep. I was a consultant, not a cop, and therefore I didn't get woken up in the middle of the night. That was more her job. She was the homicide detective.

"The department's short staffed," she said, as if it was the answer to everything. Lately, maybe it was. "This one's a priority. Listen, I can be at your apartment in sixteen. Are you going to be ready? Let me rephrase this. Be ready."

I sat up, kicked the switch on the wall with my foot that would turn off the telepathic shield generator around me. I blinked as the world turned inside out – and then Mindspace came back, full of sleeping dreams and quiet sighs.

"Why do you need me?" I asked.

"Priority case. The clock's ticking. Be ready, okay?"

I rubbed at my eyes. Sighed. "Fine."

She hung up, abrupt even for her.

"And good morning to you too," I said, and made a face. My hand went to the hidden panel in the wall, the one that held two slowly-decomposing vials of what used to be my drug. Three years clean, and I kept them there just in case, just in case I needed them. My body wrenched as I said goodbye again. Today I didn't have

1

time to fall off the wagon. Today we had a priority, whatever that meant at 3 a.m.

Then I took a quick and freezing shower, threw on clothes, and was waiting under the busted streetlight two minutes before the agreed upon time. I lit a cigarette, realized I hadn't shaved. Oh, well, at 3 a.m. probably no one would care.

"You owe me coffee," I told Cherabino grumpily, as I slid into her battered old cop car.

She handed me a ceramic lidded cup and nodded, taking in my unshaved face before deciding not to comment on it. I was dressed, after all.

Detective Isabella Cherabino was a pretty woman, tall, with dark hair, large breasts, and a black belt in something Asian and deadly. She had the highest close rate in the department, which made her a big favorite with her bosses. My help got her a big portion of those closes, so that made me a favorite with her. Well, on the days I could pull the rabbit out of the hat. On the ones I couldn't, she was insufferably grumpy until she closed the case on her own. She was a good woman, despite her flaws, someone I admired, for all her brashness. Someone I wanted to spend time with. And not just because she and this job were part of the system that kept me on the wagon, kept me fighting for the best me. Because she was Cherabino.

I hoped today was going to be a rabbit day, but half-asleep I didn't make any promises. I put on a safety belt as she pulled the car out of Park and engaged the anti-gravity generator.

I swallowed, hard, and grabbed for the handle on the door. Great. We were going to fly. My knuckles went white with the force of my grip.

Cherabino drove with her usual verve, making several highly-illegal vertical lane changes without even the benefit of a siren. I'd learned by now to stay quiet, or she'd feel like she had to make a point. I'd prefer not to throw up tonight, thank you very much. Especially not before I had to see the body. Let it not be too far gone, I prayed to the Higher Power. Also, let us not die from her driving.

In Mindspace, I felt small waves rolling off of Cherabino, focus, worry, anger, all mixed in with the odd crystal clarity of a homicide detective's work mode. Lately I tried to keep my mind to myself – she didn't like me snooping – but thinking this loudly, she wasn't making it easy.

"It's a cop," she said, words firing into the empty space of the car like bullets. She fidgeted and made another near-miss of a floating bus.

I swallowed, tried to focus on her words and not how close we'd come to dying. "Who'd he kill?"

"She," Cherabino said. "And somebody killed her, tonight. Was sitting in her backseat, waiting for her.

Strangled her to death on her way home from judo." Her mind roiled with anger, with disturbance.

Cherabino took jujitsu or something like that. She was out late, alone, a lot. She was a woman, and a cop. Like it or not, this had to be feeling real personal.

"Did you know her?" I asked.

"No," she said. "She's North DeKalb, not out of head-quarters." I could feel the effort as she pulled it together again, the measured pace of her thoughts returning with bitter force. "But she's blue. She's one of us. We bring hell to stop this guy – fast. Who knows who else he'll kill if we don't. He clearly doesn't have a fear of cops."

"If this is North DeKalb, why call us?"

"First priority," she returned. "You're the only tele-path we've got. They want you to do your juju on the crime scene, get us a name. A description. Something. No way in hell this guy walks away. Supposedly I'm your handler. When the commissioner wakes me up, I move. I don't care. Nobody kills a cop and gets away with it. Especially when we don't have a reason."

I felt her heart, beating too fast, a presence in the whole car. "Are you okay?" I asked.

"Fine."

"You're not..."

She made a face. "Ask me again when we catch this guy." She didn't like this situation. She didn't like it at all.

"Do you want me to—?"

"Shut up," she said. "You're going to pull a rabbit out of your damn hat, we're going to catch this guy, and then you can ask me whatever crappy thing you've got on your chest, okay?"

We dropped two stories as she started the grounding procedure too fast. A shriek escaped my lips. I'll admit it wasn't a manly sound, but with my life flashing before my eyes that didn't seem important.

Somehow we grounded without dying, with only a small bump, in a very dark neighborhood. As she turned the wheel and peeled us into an ancient parking garage, a blocky winding screw, level after level of concrete curled down into the ground and up into the sky. We circled up a level along the stained concrete ramp, and pulled into a circle of bright, bright lights. Row after row of police lights, flood lights, penlights, and one single, cheap car.

In the distance, a dog barked furiously.

Cherabino said hello to the detective in charge of the scene while I hung back. Detective Bull was a tall man, pale, who stood with a coiled lean power I associated with basketball. He frowned when he saw me, and checked his watch. He was angry, and nervous, and very aware of his surroundings. Cherabino and him got caught up in some kind of hail-fellow-well-met conversation, and I lost interest.

"Hello," a deep voice said from behind me.

I turned. A grizzled fifty-something uniformed cop stood there, his meaty hands tucked around his equipment belt, the right hand all too close to the gun. He was only a few inches taller than me, maybe six-one, and bulky, mixed muscle and fat. His nose had been broken multiple times. Now, he emanated strong mixed emotions, anger and worry and sorrow and guilt in a tangled, shifting knot that I found stressful to even look at.

"Hello," I responded, holding onto calm only through training and will. I upped my shields and paid more attention to the guy – a lot more attention.

"You the teep?" the cop asked gruffly.

"Telepathic expert," I corrected. "Yes, I'm him." I waited for him to pull away. Since the Tech Wars, normals feared telepaths, for good or ill. I didn't wear a patch but that didn't mean I couldn't get a face-full of that same fear.

But instead of moving away, he looked me up and down as if judging me. "What color are my boxers?"

I sighed, lowered the shields a bit, and skimmed the information off the surface of his troubled mind. Damn parlor tricks. "You wear briefs," I said. "And that was a visual I could have done without, thanks bunches." I shored up my shields, annoyed now, trying to push his nasty emotion-snarl out of my head. The fear was there all right, with anger too.

Cherabino was finishing up her conversation with the detective, maybe fifty feet away from me in front of one of the lights; she was gesturing less and looking more thoughtful, spine a little straighter. It wouldn't be long now.

So, cut to the chase. "What are you doing here?" I asked the cop.

His mouth flattened in a long line and he glanced back over at the car, currently surrounded by techs. Anger and guilt forced their way past the shields into my head. "I'm Audrey's partner."

"Your name?" I asked.

"Wiggles," he said. Stared as if he dared me to make something of it.

I swallowed a snicker. Wiggles, really?

"The station captain is a friend of mine," Wiggles said in a flat tone. "We went to academy together. I told him he should call you in."

I took a breath. Ah, the reason he was here. "I'll do everything I can," I said, very quietly.

He nodded, as if that ended the conversation. Maybe it did.

Across the parking deck in front of the lights, Bull said something to Cherabino, and left the area.

I walked closer to the crime scene, step by step. The car was a cheap domestic white box without even an anti-grav generator – strictly ground-level only, cheapest of the cheap. Cops weren't paid that well, and personal vehicles weren't covered as an additional expense, but this seemed a bit cheap even so. The car was scrupulously clean, however, from what I could see in the blinding floodlights pointed at it, with fully inflated tires and no dings.

Forensics personnel swarmed in and around the car. Their thoughts were quiet, ordered, and surface level, more than a little sleepy, and despite myself, I suppressed a yawn as I got closer. Another step, and I paused. A low-level disorder – something not right – made the little hairs on the back of my neck stand up. Someone had died here, violently and recently. I told myself not to be a ninny, that this was what I had come to see. I still shielded, hard.

Cherabino came up behind me. "Need them to move?" she asked about the techs.

I took a breath, asked myself the same question. "No, not tonight. Give me just a minute." If they'd been half as upset as Wiggles... but they weren't. It should be fine.

She fidgeted, but didn't push the issue. She let me use her as a ground when I had to drop deep into Mindspace, looking for clues. I wasn't quite ready for that, yet. I wanted to see what I could see.

A technician blocked my view of the driver's side as he took photos. Flashes of light interrupted the night until he moved away.

The driver's side window was dotted with blood, thrown onto the glass from the inside. Smears in the blood, in the window, even a crack in the safety glass, maybe from her elbow. She'd fought back.

"What was her name?" I asked.

"Audrey Peeler. Officer Peeler," Cherabino's voice said from behind me. "Hey!" she yelled. "You done with the photos already? We need the telepath to scout it."

The photographer bitched but finally moved. Then I was close enough to see it. Her. Audrey. For the first time.

Tightly-braided hair crowned her head, freckled face thrown back, hands askew. Face twisted in shock, wrenched in anger, the whites of the eyes red with blood, dark spots around them. And a long, dark red, thick line bisecting her neck, spilling dried blood down onto her shirt in irregular splotches. A thin cord in the middle of it, as transparent as fishing line, draped over the back-side of the driver's seat. A key ring, a can of pepper spray lay on the floorboards, just barely out of reach. A strap thingie on the seatbelt on the passenger's side, an ad-juster of some kind, I noticed. Not currently in use.

I sniffed. Strong smell of urine, of drying blood, stom-ach acid, violence and death. No pepper spray.

Cherabino pushed me aside, not hard, and knelt to get a better look at the woman's hands.

"Her fingers are cut to hell. Maybe got them under the cord before..." She straightened, adjusted her gloves. "Well, it wasn't enough."

Blood droplets covered the entire driver's side win-dow and part of the back window besides, lighter – a lot lighter – in the back. She must have struggled hard to send this much of her blood flying around. But a portion of the back left seat was clear of blood. And the front passenger seat was oddly clear as well, all except for that adjuster. I didn't know much about blood splatter, but the back seat had to be where the killer was when he was strangling her. The front seat...?

"Can we get on with this?" Cherabino asked. "People are waiting."

I realized the tech working on the back seat was leaving, and no one else was coming toward the car. Huh. Cherabino's yelling must have done the trick, even if I didn't strictly need them to desert the scene this time.

I slowly thinned my shields, easing into Mindspace. Cherabino held out a mental "hand" impatiently.

I held on, keeping my hands and mind to myself, and solidified my link back to the real world.

Then I dropped into Mindspace, the real world greying out as I went deeper, and deeper, my connection with Cherabino trailing out behind me like a bright yellow cord, yellow where no yellow could be. Mindspace was cloudy tonight, wrenched by wild and strong emotions, panic and blood. I rode out the panic, the suffocating panic, pain, and despair, letting them wash over me like water from a duck's back, and took a closer look.

Like a black hole, a small spot in front of me was quietly swallowing space around it, slowly, slowly. If I wasn't careful I could Fall In. Find myself trapped in whatever place minds went when they died, and die myself.

Above me, Cherabino murmured a question, the sounds flowing quietly like a stream.

"Six hours," I guessed, hoping the question was what I thought it was. "The M.E. can tell you that, probably. And yes, it was a violent death, here. She was killed here, and the killer..." I went looking for his signature, for his feelings left over in Mindspace like thin ghosts. "Her panic is strong. She didn't know her killer. And he... it's definitely a he. He's very quiet. Very calm, with a sharp... a sharp something to him. I'm not sure I would know him again if you put him in front of me. Her panic is just too strong."

I moved around that center black hole, slowly, taking care not to disturb what I was looking at. I wanted a better look at the killer, I think.

But there, on the other side of the woman's panicked emotion-ghosts, on the other side of her death, were the emotions of another mind, someone else who'd been here, in the car. A small, terrified person whose panic had mixed in with the cop's so that I hadn't seen him at first.

I squelched my strong, emotional reaction as too dangerous, too destructive in Mindspace. When I was calm, I surfaced.

I opened my eyes and saw the real world.

"There was a kid," I told Cherabino. "A kid. Maybe four, five, six years old, and he ran away, fast. He might still be here."

Shock, concern, disbelief radiated off her in waves, but I was already rushing around the car, dodging techs and cops, following the boy's frightened mind-trace like a bloodhound.

The sound of squealing tires echoed behind me, along with yelling from the cops as some pedestrian tried to get in the garage. The dog still barked, somewhere out there. And one scared little boy, hours ago, had run as fast as his small feet could have taken him, falling twice, the pain and frustration of each fall blooming like terrified flowers in the fabric of Mindspace.

I ran, half blind to the real world, distantly noting that I would look like a fool to the cops and not entirely sure I cared right now.

Because the killer had been this way, too, or someone had, someone calm, sharp, and annoyed. And I had to find the boy before he did.

Away from the lights, the parking garage was a dark cavern of concrete, painted lines, and forgotten cars full of shadows and emotion-ghosts. With me skimming along the surface of Mindspace, I could see assignations, drug deals, moments of worry over lost cars layered upon layered in deep, textured dark. Months of memories. Months. Far more than usual. Mindspace here was deep, and eager to learn.

In the dark, surrounded by sharp memories and the sour taste of fear, the parking deck seemed like a deadly carnival ride, something I couldn't step off of. I was here for a kid, I told myself. And I'd see the killer coming – I'd see his mind. There was nothing to fear.

But, as a shadow moved, I knew I was kidding myself. I had to push on anyway, my heart beating too fast, my body starting at every change. Concentrate on the kid's trail, I told myself. The kid.

The taste of his fear wandered down the line of cars in a staggering path. Here, a level below where we had been, a level down the sloping concrete into the bowels of the earth, the kid slowed.

Mommy! His thoughts echoed off the cold walls. *Mommy,* it choked. The boy was afraid. Afraid of the dark. Afraid of the monster he's just seen do... something *bad.*

And the killer, growing more annoyed by the moment, followed ever after.

Down another ramp, this one more deserted, I felt the kid's trail stop, next to a tangle of pipes and a control box dominating one corner of the lot. In the barely-lit shadow, the nest of pipes looked impenetrable. The killer's trail grew thicker here, like he had stopped for a moment, for a long moment full of impatient annoyance, before he went on, before he found the elevator and his trail disappeared.

Maybe I was supposed to follow the killer, to catch this guy at any cost. But I couldn't leave the kid be.

I stood in front of the pipes, let the Mindspace there sink in, until it settled into my very bones, until I felt what the boy had felt. Until the thoughts he'd left behind became my thoughts. I was tired, overwhelming tired and scared, and I'd peed myself, not like a big boy. I was cold. And I was finally, finally sleeping. A little. I wanted my blankie. I wanted my Mommy.

With a gentle wrench, I pulled myself away – that wasn't Mindspace. That was the boy himself. His consciousness, asleep but strong. In the real world, I shifted around to the back of the tangle of pipes. There, in a small niche between two large pipes, way in the back, I saw a foot. A small foot.

The clattering of Cherabino's shoes came from above, from the curling concrete ramp above me. A radio sputtered on her hip.

Still crouched in front of the pipes, not wanting to wake the boy, I found Cherabino. Sent one, clear thought, flavored with my mind so she couldn't mistake it:

I found the boy. He's hiding.

"Stay out of my head," she said, more out of habit than conviction. Her feet sped up, coming closer.

With apologies, I pulled away.

Cherabino cursed my ancestry, then spoke into the radio: "Small child, Level Five section Four-Dee, repeat Five section Four-Dee. We need a medic." She glanced down, still thirty feet away from me. "Maybe a shrink," she said.

I stood awkwardly to the side and smoked, the sinuous trail of it winding up the open heart of the curling parking lot, smoke drifting in a long stream up into the darkness. The cops were clustered around the kid, the elevator, anything else they could get. I was pushed out, away from the action, standing in the cold central parking deck, even my cigarette butts ignored.

Cherabino didn't get ignored. She was just as much a stranger as I was in this part of the county, but she got respect. I was the expert. They'd called me in specifically. Not that it meant anything.

My first kid at a crime scene – a living one, anyway – and no one would let me do anything. I made a face and lit another cigarette.

Finally a uniformed woman cop carried the kid up the ramp, every line of her body filled with relief. The kid held onto her tightly, and shook. Wiggles trailed behind them.

"For gods' sake, put the cigarette out," he told me. "He's a kid."

I sighed and snubbed out the blue cigarette under my shoe. At least the little guy seemed okay.

Wiggles kept moving, concern leaking out behind him in a long trail, and Cherabino walked up behind me. She was exhausted, now that the adrenaline had passed, and cranky.

She worried about her knees, which hurt from crouching on the concrete trying to get the boy to trust her. And of course in the end, he'd come out for the uniformed cop, not her. Maybe the woman had looked more like his mother. But her knees hurt and she was cranky anyway.

"You could have given me one," she said, and I had to figure out what she was talking about.

I pulled out the half-empty pack of blue cigarettes and the lighter, handed them over.

"Give it a minute," I said. "Until the kid's gone." With the kid gone, Wiggles could deal with the smoke.

She held the pack, sighed, but didn't light up. "Tell me about the killer," she said. "Not the path he took – you pointed that out to the techs, I'm sure they'll do fine. About the killer, as a person. Give me something I can use to catch this guy."

I looked over at the clump of North DeKalb cops talking to a secondary detective over on the other side of the deck. "I'm not a cop," I said, "but shouldn't we be over there? With them?"

Cherabino shrugged. "They don't trust you." She lit a cigarette, hands sure on the lighter as if this was a completely normal statement. Maybe to her it was.

"Telepath thing?" I asked. Since the Tech Wars, when the Telepath's Guild had stepped up to save the world – and gotten real scary to do it – a lot of the normals didn't trust telepaths. Even seventy years later. I hoped at least this time it wasn't personal against me, drug problem, felon, or not. I mean, they didn't know me well enough to hate me yet.

She nodded, shrugged. "You were telling me about the killer. Something I can use to lock him up."

"This isn't your case?"

"The killer," she said, circles under her eyes seeming to grow even deeper.

I closed my eyes to recall what I'd seen in Mindspace. Tried to tease out details that would help her. "A man. Not old, not young. Confidant. Calm. He's killed before – he's killed that way before. No fumbling, no worry about details. I'm not sure he saw the kid. If he did, it didn't break the calm. He chased after the boy – to take care of witnesses, perhaps? – annoyed when he had to go farther than he expected. I didn't get a read of any purpose other than the killing itself, though with the woman's panic—"

"Audrey," Cherabino corrected. "Officer Peeler's panic. At being strangled to death. While fighting back. Tell me something that will catch this guy. What he looks like, maybe. That'd be a good start."

I shuffled through impressions, memories. The woman hadn't seen her killer – she'd been strangled from the back and had other things on her mind other than looking calmly in the rearview mirror. The killer hadn't sat around and thought emotion-drenched thoughts about what he looked like. And with all the adult emotion in the car, I'd hardly felt the kid there at all.

Apparently I was silent too long, because Cherabino said, "Well, you did what you could, I guess."

"We can go back to the car," I said defensively. "I'll know better what I'm looking at this time. Maybe..."

Cherabino sighed. "They'll be here for hours, going over every spot of physical evidence. Do you really think you'll get something new?"

I paused. "Well, no."

"Then we're leaving," she said. "I've got an early morning tomorrow, and I need at least a little sleep."

"Don't we have to...?"

"It's not my case," Cherabino said, pragmatically.

I spent the day firmly ensconced in the interview room, talking to guilty defensive suspects and stupid defensive witnesses with spotty memories. I'd had an early-morning meeting with my Narcotics Anonymous sponsor and no additional sleep. I felt like I was running on empty, past empty, until my internal gears scraped together.

I was supposed to be talking to a local drug pusher, but I got the call to go upstairs instead. I blinked at the messenger, hardly able to process the request. "Fine," I said. "Give me a minute."

Paulsen – my boss – was sitting at her desk, her office empty except for its usual snowstorm of papers. She was a young sixty-something Black woman with high standards. Standards, as she put it, that she expected to be met.

"What is it now?" I asked.

Her eyes flashed. "Now, you'll go back into that head of yours and remember I'm your boss. The key to your continued job security."

I took a breath. Rubbed my eyes. I needed a nap, bad. "I'll rephrase then. What exciting assignment do you have for me today?"

She let it go, pushing some papers to the side of her desk. "North DeKalb is asking for you again. As I don't want a cop killer roaming the streets, I've said yes. Cherabino will take you. I'd suggest you get ready."

I frowned. "They didn't seem to like me at the scene last night. And the scene will be even less substantial this morning."

"Liking has nothing to do with it," she said, firmly.

"What will I be doing?"

"They didn't say." She met my eyes. "Now, get packed."

I sighed. More work. Peachy.

Cherabino was unusually quiet on the drive to North DeKalb, her driving – for her – relatively sane. Tired focus leaked from her, and I noticed her hands shaking, her breathing just a little fast like she'd had far too much coffee.

"Where are we going?" I asked, to distract myself from the craving. They said in the Program if you distracted yourself, you wouldn't want it anymore. Sometimes it was true. Today maybe I was tired enough for it to be true.

"Audrey's house," Cherabino said. From the case in the parking garage, her mind supplied.

"Why go to the house?" I asked. No one had died in the house, had they? I felt like I was missing something, brain not quite tracking.

"Not sure," she said, and would say nothing else. Since she spent the rest of the trip thinking about an unrelated shooting case, I couldn't even steal it from her thoughts. Assuming she was even lying. Maybe she didn't know. I wondered even so.

I mean, I'd as much as told her yesterday that the guy was a professional. I would have laid money on him being a hitman, a murder-for-hire guy. At the least, ex-military. It was hard to be that cold while killing; it took a lot of practice and a lot of confidence. I didn't see where going to the house was going to get us to the hitman. Maybe they were just chasing down leads. Either way seemed dumb to invite me, but hey, if they were willing to pay the fees, the Homicide department needed the money.

Twenty minutes later, Cherabino touched the car down onto a small residential street, most of the homes small, with native red brick and small shrubs. Two lots were taken over with mammoth twenty-first century mansions, built right up to the property line. The wood on those was blackened, the porches starting to sag despite many artificial supports and a fresh paint job. The small brick houses still stood as strong as they had a hundred years ago; progress was overrated, apparently.

The house we wanted was a slightly-larger version of the same modest brick ranch style house, complete with carport and carefully-trimmed shrubs. Brightly colored toys were strewn about the front yard, one stuffed rabbit still soaked from last night's rain. It would mold if someone didn't bring it inside, I thought.

We got out of the car and crossed to the front door, using the sidewalk. From inside, I could hear a baby crying. I braced myself, building heavy shields to keep me from the despair already wafting from the house. This would not be fun.

Wiggles opened the door. When he saw Cherabino, he waved her in. Me he addressed cautiously. "Walk careful."

"I understand," I said, in a careful, calm tone. No need to get anyone any more upset than they already were. The sound of baby crying came louder from deeper in the house.

He closed the door behind us. "Jake's in the kitchen."

Cherabino nodded. "Anything we should focus on?" She wasn't quite sure why she was there, but trying to bluff her way out. I sat back and let it happen; she was better in this environment than I was.

Wiggles nodded, slow. "Jake won't say anything. And we need an ID, ASAP."

"He's five," Cherabino said quietly. "Maybe you should give him some time."

"I know he's five, dammit. He's my partner's kid. But I'll be damned if I let her killer walk away from this. He's not talking to George. He's not talking to me." He looked at me. "We need him to talk, and you're the logical choice."

"You want me to read the kid's mind," I said, finally putting two and two together.

"That's what I said."

Great. I took a breath. "Legally, I can't read a child under the age of thirteen without his express consent," I said. "Unless he's in real physical or emotional danger, or a measurable telepath. Privacy laws."

"Audrey's killer is out there. Walking the streets. A cop killer, you understand. A cop killer."

People kept saying that, like it was a mantra. "It doesn't change the law," I said.

Wiggles's anger swelled like a tidal wave. Cherabino grabbed my arm and pulled me into a side hallway. The ugly architectural wallpaper was faded from age.

"Could you not be difficult right now?" she hissed. "This is a cop's worst nightmare, and you're just making it worse for him."

"I'll talk to the kid," I said. "I never said I wouldn't." Then, after a second: "He seems awfully attached for someone who's just a partner."

"A partner's everything on the beat," she said. "You spend more time with them than your family, you fight together, you trust them with your life."

"But she's a woman, and he's, well... not dead." I said. "There has to be some level of sexual tension, or feelings, or something."

"Some of the older guys say women partners are better," she said, defensively. "The adrenaline cycles are different, so someone's always thinking, always thinking somewhere in the fight. Plus one tear isn't going to get you screwed over." Her mind added: why the younger guys were so macho, why they couldn't get their shit together... (and why she couldn't find herself a stable partner...)

I reined myself in, refusing to respond to the stability comment even though I wanted to. I wasn't supposed to be reading her anyway. Distantly, I heard the far-off baby stop crying. I was still holding out reservations about Wiggles and the partnership.

She looked down, and I noticed the painful wallpaper again. She considered not telling me what she'd found out, decided I needed to know. She leaned forward, close, very close. The edge of her presence in Mindspace brushed against me like silk.

Her breath touched my ear. "Audrey had a Narcotics case undercover a while ago. A couple of big enemies on the street. But, she just testified in a case against a former lottery official. An official who's Wiggle's cousin. He's a clean cop, by all the records. A good guy. It doesn't necessary mean anything."

She paused, her breath tickling my ear, painfully close. "Be gentle with Jake. He could act younger than he is. He could do – well, anything. Don't make it worse."

"I understand," I said, smelling the closeness of her hair. Something inside me mourned as she stepped away.

Two more cops were standing in the Peelers' small living room, Detective Bull and another guy from last night. Both were distrustful of me, but Bull was also nervous. I paused in the living room, Cherabino and Wiggles following me. It seemed strange he was nervous.

"I need to go," Bull said, firmly. He turned to the back door.

Wiggles was suddenly beside him. "No," he said with punch. "No, stay."

Bull looked at him, wary, trying to figure out how to leave the sticky situation, angry he had to be here at all.

And Wiggles was mad, mad and guilty.

"What's going on?" I asked, words echoing into the awkwardness. As soon as the words were out of my mouth I regretted them.

But I was closer to Wiggles, closer and I'd read him once already this afternoon. I saw the trail his thoughts made – his instinctual answer to the question. I dipped in and stole them.

Huh. I'd expected a power play, the uniformed cop who'd never been promoted angry at the detective a decade his junior. Instead what I got was a rivalry, a rivalry with a woman at its center – Audrey Peeler. Bull and she had been lovers.

No one responded to my words, but they hung in the air like lead weights, making everything more intense.

Some twist of guilt rolled in Wiggles's gut, a twist that made him even more angry, and he grabbed Bull's arm. "You're not going anywhere until the teep reads Jake," he said. "It's the least you can do, after..."

Bull stared Wiggles down. Wiggles slowly removed his arm, frustration painting the air like sparklers.

Hmm. There was something there. Something deeper than was obvious.

"Jake's in the kitchen," Wiggles said, still standing far too close to Bull. "Jake's in the kitchen," he repeated, now clearly to me.

I took my cue.

The small eat-in was decked with more brightly-colored ugly wallpaper meant to mimic blueprints. The heavy-lined background made the walls dance to the eyes, and made me nauseated. Worse was the teeth-jarring high-pitched buzzing in Mindspace that I could feel as I got closer.

"You have a quantum stasis box?" I forced out. They were easily ten times the cost of a fridge – and a waste of money. The electromagnetic field they generated as a side effect also interacted with Mindspace in a way that was already giving me a headache.

I assumed the man in the kitchen was George, Peeler's husband. He looked absent, like he was in shock. He nodded to me – after a long moment of delay – with an empty look. He was average looking in every way, medium complexion with messy hair, wearing a wrinkled button-up shirt and juggling a baby, a toy, a jar of peanut butter, and overwhelming confused grief. The baby, maybe six months old, was hiccupping quietly.

At the kitchen table next to them, a boy of five – the same boy from last night – was chewing slowly on a peanut butter sandwich. He didn't look at me. He didn't look at anyone.

"Can you turn off the stasis box?" I prompted. Thank God they were expensive enough to be rare. Keeping meat in stasis would make it last practically forever, sure. But if you actually ate your food, you didn't need it to last forever. You needed it to last two days. The fact that the family had one of these and Peeler had driven a crap car said bad things about the couple's relationship. Priorities all out of whack. Plus an annoyance to me, an annoyance that would keep me from doing my job if it didn't get shut off.

When the man just looked at me, I walked over – the pain getting stronger with every step – and flipped the switch myself.

"Mr. Peeler," I said.

He looked at me for a moment with dead eyes, then the baby hiccupped again. "George," he said. Uncomfortable baby thoughts floated across the room, underscored by his complex grief.

I nodded. "I'm a Level Eight telepath. The department sent me over. Do you mind if I talk to your son?"

"Why?"

I took a breath, reminded myself to be patient. I could afford to be patient; let's face it, this wasn't going to be fun. Watching a five year old's view of his mother dying did not sound good.

"He might have seen something that will help us find your wife's killer," I said.

George winced, looked away. Then back at me. "I'll have to be here," he said. "If he gets upset, it's over." Grief came off of him in waves.

"I understand," I said, in my best soothing voice, not that I expected it to do anything but keep the situation from getting worse. With the baby there I didn't want to project anything emotional.

I felt Cherabino's mind settle behind me, Wiggles following. She was maybe standing right outside the kitchen. "Be careful," she murmured.

I took a breath and sat down at the table with the kid. He drew back from me, the remaining bite of the peanut butter sandwich dropping to the floor.

"You probably don't remember me," I said quietly, trying not to be scary. "But I was there last night, with the police. I'd like to talk to you about what happened."

I wasn't good with kids, even when I'd been one, and the Guild didn't get anyone until they were at least nine or ten. Five was very young, much younger than I knew what to do with.

Vague thoughts like blobby birds flitted across his mind, with strong snaking emotions. That was all I could see and still keep my distance in Mindspace; I would give him space, unless he gave me permission.

The kid looked at his dad, who nodded encouragement. Then he looked back at me. His energy was wary.

"I'd like to talk to you about what happened," I said. "I'd like, if you'll let me, to help you remember."

He looked away. Climbed down to the floor, going after the leftover peanut butter sandwich.

The dad looked on suspiciously as I moved down to floor level as well. I sat down where the dad could see both me and the kid clearly. Then I tried to figure out what the next step was.

The kid put the bite of sandwich in his mouth, chewing messily, peanut butter leaking out – he pushed it back in with a hand. A smear of it and purple jelly sat on the floor. He didn't look at me.

Well, this wasn't going very well. Maybe he needed a minute, to see I was okay. But the dad was looking at me closely, and I just didn't have the patience to sit on a dirty floor for hours. Time to ask the question a different way.

"We need your help," I told the kid. "The bad man – we're going to find him and lock him away. But I need access to your memories – I need you to remember."

The kid looked up, a small glance, then another. He smeared the peanut butter across the floor.

I waited. Finally I prompted: "the bad man?"

"Will he hurt me now?" the boy said very, very quietly.

"We'll find him," I promised, hoping it was true. "He won't hurt anyone ever again. Not anymore. We've got a lot of strong, clever policemen who will make sure he won't." I paused. "Do you know what a telepath is?"

The boy frowned. He looked at his dad, who made a gesture. Then he looked back at me. "Someone who can see... in your head... like a lightbulb."

Not a bad comparison, actually. "Yes. I'd like you to let me see in your head so we can get more information about the bad man."

"My head?" he looked disturbed at the concept, which was both good news and bad news for me. Good news because it was clear he understood what I was asking. Bad because, well, he didn't have to agree.

"No," he said.

Wiggles came into the kitchen like an emotional cloud of mustard gas covering everything I could see. Jake looked up, way up. Wiggles scooped up the boy in his arms, and I bit my tongue shoring up shields hurriedly against the Mindspace pollution.

Cherabino, Bull, and the other cop were now standing around the doorway to the kitchen. The baby had started to cry again, little whimpers the father was struggling to soothe. Feeling very vulnerable at floor level, I struggled to my feet, my lungs panting a little from the cigarettes.

The boy's body language melted into Wiggles's arms, trust, and he started to suck his thumb.

Wiggles pulled the thumb out of the little boy's mouth gently. "Now, you need to talk to the telepath here." He shifted the boy's weight. "It's really important."

The baby started screaming, and I winced.

Jake put his thumb back in his mouth and shook his head. Great. I had a second 'no.' Legally and ethically, I couldn't ignore it.

Of course I had to pick now to have scruples, when not less than four cops and a concerned dad were staring at me. When everything was riding on what this kid knew. I had to pick *now* to have ethics. I sighed. "No. No I can't do that. He's a kid. He's clearly said no, and I have to respect his decision. He's been through something probably none of us here in the room can imagine – I'm not going to push him to go through something he doesn't want."

Various levels of shock and disapproval emanated from the adults in the room and Jake burrowed deeper into Wiggles's shoulder. Cherabino's mouth set in a hard line. Cop killer, her mind flashed at me. We have to find the cop killer. It could have been her. The baby screamed like the end of the world had come, and I winced.

"This is a waste of time," Bull said, loud enough to be heard over the baby. His tone was combative and angry, but an odd sense of relief came off of him in Mindspace.

And that relief seemed wrong.

"If Jake doesn't want it, we're not going to do it," George said, in the distracted-but-firm tone of a guy dealing with screaming in one hand and reality in the other.

Wiggles's mouth pressed into a hard line. "Where are you going?" he asked Bull, who had turned. His voice cracked hard, like a whip.

Bull stood up straight – tall, much taller than anyone else in the room. "This is a waste of time," he said. "There's work to do and I'm not standing here while the real work sits by." And again, the strong sense of relief came off him, relief and vindication. He turned and walked out – with Wiggles close behind him.

Never one to give up a free show, I followed. Cherabino and Bull's partner completed the set, as we walked through the living room, outside the front door, and out to the lawn, where the damp stuffed rabbit was molding from the rain.

Wiggles stood in front of Bull, blocking his way on the sidewalk. Bull, jaw hard, moved past him.

Wiggles grabbed his arm again to stop him. "Your dicking around caused this. If George hadn't—"

"Let go of my arm," Bull said, his hand on his gun. "Now." His partner stood up behind him.

Wiggles dropped the arm but didn't move out of the way. "If they hadn't been on the rocks, Jake wouldn't have been there."

Regret like shadows passed across Bull's face. "That was not - Jake's not a bad kid. He shouldn't have been there." He glanced around, saw me. Went back to Wiggles. "Looks like your teep didn't do crap for you." A pause. "It's time for you to give it up and come do real work." He was so guarded – too guarded – so that I couldn't get any read from him except that odd sense of relief.

Something smelled off about the situation, and my instincts from the interview room came out in full force.

Just to see what would happen, I twisted the tiger's tail. "You mean like financial records? The killer was a professional; odds are the guy who hired him was close to her. We could go over everyone's financial records, see if George is holding out on us. See if you guys are holding out on us."

"Are you really accusing officers of being involved?" Bull spat. Anger came from nearly everyone in the room.

Their anger and distaste hung in the air, then Wiggles shrugged. "An accountant's not a bad idea."

Bull's partner, a short man, frowned. "If you need to eliminate suspects, do it, but don't slow the real work down. We've got limited time to find this guy. He could already be on his way out of town if he's really a gunman."

"This is a waste of time," Bull said, mind still guarded, closed. "Peeler had eighteen cases still in court. Two of them grand theft auto – one from Gwinnett. Maybe she picked up the wrong car, got Fiske's attention. Annoyed somebody with powerful friends. Everybody knows cops don't hire killers."

Cops don't hire killers? The words were out of place, like a yellow flashing light above his head.

I smiled. Looks like I would get my rabbit trick after all. Next to me, Cherabino frowned, thinking.

"I'm a Level Eight telepath," I told Bull. "Do you know what that means?"

"What?"

"It means I know the truth," I riffed. Interviewers could bluff; in fact it was encouraged. I could almost see the blocky table between us.

"What are you getting at?" Bull's partner asked.

Bull's eyes darted between me and Cherabino, Wiggles and his partner. The partner took a step back, tension in the air confusing him. Bull said, "I was just saying, cops don't hire killers."

"But you did," I said, certainty riding every syllable. "You hired someone you knew, someone you knew would put us off your trail. You hired him to strangle her in a bad part of town. But you didn't know the kid would be there."

Bull took a step back; I stepped forward. His hand went for his gun; I prepared my mind to dart in and hold him immobile. One gun wasn't a threat to me, not holstered; I could shut down his movements before he could pull the trigger. I enveloped his mind in Mindspace, prepared...

"This is ridiculous," Bull's partner said. "Your teep is smoking something."

"Cops don't hire killers," Bull repeated, like a mantra. He didn't say he didn't do it; he couldn't. Faced with the certainty of a telepath and a lie, he just couldn't say it.

"Give me your gun," Wiggles said, his voice cracking like a whip.

"This is ridiculous," the partner repeated, his voice suddenly wavering. He looked back and forth between them.

"The kid's mine," Bull said, angry tone. "Not Jake, the baby. The baby that fucker named Georgette. What kind of crap name is Georgette?" And his mind opened one, small degree, his panicked motivation falling out like a candy from a dispenser.

And the rabbit trick arrived – I knew how to get the confession. "She was going to transfer," I said. "Move halfway across the country. And tell the truth about your secret."

"The baby's not a secret," Wiggles said. "Even George knows. Not that this dick knows anything about loyalty."

My eyes stayed on Bull. "That's not the secret."

Now he took three steps back, four, terror and shame coming from him in tidal waves. His hand went to his gun – and I swooped in.

His fingers were frozen, gun halfway from his holster. His mind was terrified. And, in a pocket of quiet time,

I spoke to him: *Tell the truth about what happened. Tell the truth or I'll tell them how you cheated on your detective exams. I'll go into details.*

It was Bull's one, horrible secret. The one thing he that shamed of more than any other – and the one thing that would strip him of everything he loved. Also the only detail I could corroborate on my own – that, I could prove, without a doubt, from the record.

I held onto his hands, keeping them frozen like heavy blocks out of his control. But, one small step at a time, I let go of the rest of him – including his mouth.

"Tell them or I will," I said.

In my periphery, I saw Wiggles go for his own gun, Cherabino for hers in return. The partner was stepping away, stepping away.

"Let go of him," Wiggles said, fear in his voice. "You're..."

"Tell them." My voice was implacable. But my mind was gentle, no suggestions, no coercion. My heart beat hard; I wouldn't be able to stop Wiggles from shooting me, not like this. "Tell them, okay?"

Bull collapsed in on himself. "She was going to tell."

I waited, and Wiggles's gun wavered.

"She was going to tell them. Said I was a bastard, that I couldn't see the kid, not anymore. And... so I asked for an introduction. I paid him. And he said he'd take care of it. Jake wasn't supposed to be there." He looked up, at Wiggles. "I swear to you, Jake wasn't supposed to be there." Guilt rolled over him for that, but even still, all he felt for his former lover was... anger.

I'd had a lover betray me too, once. I understood – to a point. I hadn't killed Kara. And she hadn't been married.

"Take his gun," I told Cherabino, focus still on Bull, mind still holding. "Careful of his hands, they'll be stiff."

The partner stood in her way, confused but standing up against the outsider.

"It was you?" Wiggles asked, voice intense. He thought about shooting Bull – thought hard enough I let go of the hold on Bull's mind – but instead, Wiggles hit him hard across the face with the butt of his gun.

Pain echoed in Mindspace, and Bull fell over. His gun, in front of him.

Wiggles picked it up. "What's the secret?" he asked me, his own gun not pointing at me anymore, but the threat still there.

I was silent.

"Damn teeps." He shook his head, disgusted. Looked at Bull's partner. "You going to read him the rights or should I?" he asked.

Bull's partner sighed. "I'll do it."

"The killer was definitely a professional," Cherabino said, over a huge container of pasta in the department break room that night. "He's been linked to at least six other cases in the metro area." Day shift was over, and we'd ordered Italian takeout. Or, more accurately, I'd ordered it for us both, the good stuff, the expensive stuff with real meat. It was heaven on a plate.

"How did Bull meet him?" I asked. "I mean, you don't get a list of hired killers when you join the department." I tried again to cut the osso bucco with the plastic knife without tearing the cardboard box it had come in. I managed one, small, strip of meat and sighed.

Cherabino finished chewing and shrugged. "Guess he knew a snitch with a connection. We'll find the hired gun eventually."

I speared a roasted potato wedge with the plastic fork. When it fell off, speared it again, more carefully. "I still can't get over the fact that he hired someone else to kill her. I mean, I get it. Someone leaves you, you're angry. I've been there. But killing the woman? Or, that whole extra step of getting someone else to do it? How do you get that far down the road?"

She looked down at her plate, sadness, pain and cynicism mixing around in her head. "It's a damn stupid thing to do. I went to academy with that guy – I didn't think he could..." She trailed off. "What was his secret?"

I was silent.

"You're not going to tell me, are you?"

"Compared to murder, it doesn't matter," I said.

"I guess you never really know someone." She looked sad, incredibly sad in that moment, and the emotions inside her cut through me like a one-two punch. Maybe I shouldn't have said anything...

"There's one garlic roll left," I told her, desperately. "It's yours if you want it." I pushed the cardboard container towards her.

She took the roll, and started talking about another case. This one about industrial sabotage. I listened carefully and asked lots of questions. And slowly, like the release of a long-held tension, her mind calmed.

I looked up as Paulsen came in the door. "Oh, good," she said with a smile. "You're still here."

I ate another potato with dogged determination. If I was going to be working a double, I'd need the energy.

Turn the page for
two bonus short stories
in new worlds
by Alex Hughes

The Carousel

By Alex Hughes

Behind me, the empty carousel rotated, the figures inside imprisoned in an endless loop.

"Excuse me?"

I glanced up from the magazine. Turned.

A small child looked up at me with big eyes. "Can I ride the horsies?" Behind her, a tired mother stood with a stroller.

Great. Another one. "No, you can't. We're closed."

"It's rotating," the mother said in a quiet voice.

"Horsies! I want the horsies!" the little girl said, looking at the nursery rhyme characters with their brass detailing like the carousel was made of jelly beans.

I put the magazine to the side, my stomach sinking. "There aren't any horsies here, see? Just ducks and nursery rhyme characters. For babies. You don't want to be a baby, do you?"

As I spoke, to the right Bo Peep's eyes glinted at me.

"Not a baby!" The kid screwed up her face.

I held out a hand, still keeping an eye on Bo Peep. "Don't cry."

The mother had already found the unsteady bench the mall stocked for parents that never came. "Can't she just ride for awhile?"

"It's fifteen dollars." I needed her to go away.

The mother's brow creased. Finally. The carousel was empty for a reason.

But the little girl jumped up and down. "Please please please please please?"

The mother shook her head, her blonde hair disheveled. Then she pulled out a worn wallet.

I looked at the creased bills. The rules said I couldn't stop them if they were really determined. But: "You assume all responsibility for the risk," I told the mom as sternly as I could. Inside, my stomach fluttered. It had been months...

She sighed, nodded, and started to push the stroller back and forth to soothe the hiccuping baby within.

I knew the rules. Unlocking the controls, I slowed the carousel, the shiny ducks and sheep turning slower and slower, while Mother Goose glared above them all. When the platform was still I opened the gate – it protested with a low, solid creak.

The girl shot through like a released dove, her little legs moving so fast they blurred. She looked up at Miss Muffet and the spider beside her. "What's dat?"

I didn't say anything. I couldn't influence the choice, and Muffet wasn't so bad. As it went.

But the little girl looked with wide eyes and staggered around the edge – past Peter Piper. Past Jack Horner. Right to the grimly smiling Bo Peep and her retinue of sharp-toothed sheep.

The little girl's eyes widened with wonder, as if she was looking at something beyond the plaster, bronze and paint in front of me. "Up!"

Bo Peep, huh? I felt like throwing up, but I raised the girl to the seat on Peep's skirts. I set her down carefully, got her situated in the plaster. "Hold on," I told her seriously, quietly.

Then, watching the girl with a heavy heart, I turned on the carousel.

Tinkling music swelled as the figures turned, faster and faster. The little girl squealed as she went past, and Bo Peep smiled ominously.

The mother, oblivious, rocked her baby back and forth in the stroller. Every line in the mother's body was tired, worn, as worn as the figures on the carousel. The tinkling music played, echoing off the walls of the empty mall.

My hand shook over the "off" button, but I knew the rules. The girl went past me, once, twice, three times.

And this time I saw it happen. Bo Peep's skirts snapped up and swooshed around the girl in an unbreakable hold. The girl shrieked in terror – and in the space of a second, froze solid, her skin ashen. The skirts crept up like the sides of a pitcher plant on a fly, enveloping the terrified girl in gilded plaster.

The carousel turned, the animals went up and down along their endless track while the music played. And quietly, without ceremony, the lump on the back of Bo Peep got smaller and smaller.

Three minutes later, I stopped the empty carousel. I knew the rules.

I wouldn't tell the mother yet, though, I thought as I watched her tiredly move the stroller back and forth. Not yet.

Inky Black Sea

By Alex Hughes

On the deck of the schooner *Josephina*, fifty-five-year-old Captain Allende looked out over the waters near Cape Verde and wondered how he would survive as a landsman. It was to be his last journey, God and His Majesty decreeing that sailors should return to shore in old age. He didn't feel so old, for all his body creaked with the creaking of the ship. He didn't feel so old he must give up everything he'd ever known, not so old he must leave off adventures and joy. But most of his brethren died at two-score years, and His Majesty's decree was law.

Sailors darted around him in every direction, and he kept an eye on the first mate. Ortiz handled the ship well, the sailors respecting him. He would make a fine captain. If Allende had to give up his ship to anyone, it would be Ortiz. But the loss of it sat in his chest like a bird in a cage, small and shivering.

The sea was choppy today, with a dark tinge underneath like the ink of some terrible monster released out into the deep. In forty years at sea, Allende had never seen such a color on the ocean, not even here, off the coast of Africa. Many a ship had disappeared in this area of the world, and he was superstitious enough to wonder if the color of the sea had aught to do with it. The ink-black ebbed and flowed, back and forth, as if it sat on the surface of the waves. He watched the horizon with the sextant, praying they would arrive safe at their destination, and yet praying in his heart of hearts they would tarry just a day longer, just a week longer, on the sea.

The jangling boot-steps of the nobleman stomped towards him. Allende braced himself before turning.

Allende bowed slightly to the man, a gesture of respect he felt he had not earned. "de Tera. I trust you enjoy the journey?" Dressed in finery from His Majesty's court directly and a known supporter of the Inquisition, de Tera was an irritant at best and dangerous at worst. He must be treated gently, for all Allende wished to throw him in the sea a hundred times over.

"You should not have taken him onboard," de Tera said, too loudly, across the deck where any common sailor could hear. "The Venetians are known consorters with magicians. You risk the wrath of God on this journey. And His Majesty's wrath as well."

"We have discussed the issue yet," Allende returned after taking a few steps forward, his voice pitched more quietly so as not to carry. "The Venetian carries recommendations from a cardinal and more than enough money to justify his place. His port is a scant two days' journey away now. There seems little point in debating what will soon be over. Besides, he is below, praying. Surely even you cannot object to a pious man."

"You can still throw him overboard," de Tera pressed, viciously. "If he is innocent, he will float. If he is guilty of foul magics, he will sink like a stone and cease to bother the rest of us. God says you shall allow no hint—"

"It is two days' journey," the captain interrupted, his voice a little too passionate. He paused, and chose a more even tone. Reason must stand against even the blood-stirred Inquisition. "Noble sir, the agreement is long since made. Shall I become an oathbreaker? Shall that please God? Save have a little patience, and we will leave him at his destination to not trouble us again." But his eyes returned to the waves, calming now. The ink-black color grew stronger to the eye.

de Tera opened his mouth to protest again, but the first mate came with a question regarding course, and Allende chose to busy himself overmuch in its details.

Suddenly a cry came from the mast. "Ahead! Ahead!"

Allende moved to the very edge of the helm, looking out. There—in the distance—a cloud like a herd of galloping animals, throwing up dust above the sea against all reason.

"Pray get below deck," he told de Tera.

"I will not move until you have answered—"

"Get below!" he interrupted, a tinge of panic in his voice despite his best efforts. The cloud was closing fast, far faster than the fastest ship in the armada, terrifying in its speed.

The wind died. Sailors stopped in their tracks, and an officer screamed. The crack of a whip, and movement again on the deck. de Tera stood and stared.

The ship slowed, hitching forward and back in a way that defied all nature. The sea grew black, black as thick ink from any nobleman's pot, and the waves disappeared. The ship slowed further, lurching in the now-viscous sea, thicker than honey, impossible to sail.

The cloud was right on top of them. Lightning crashed.

And then the fog dissipated, revealing the terrible visage of a monster. Its face was as large as a sail, its teeth larger than a man, and its matted hair fell behind it, disappearing into the ink-sea as its body did. An almost-human body, it was, with scales covering it, a female body.

Men stared, and cried out. Some fell on the deck, prostrated. de Tera crossed himself and began to chant in low tones, fingers white on his rosary.

Allende—and the sailors—waited for death. But the monster did nothing. Minutes passed, as de Tera's chant increased, and the sailors' superstitions built. One cried out that this was the Venetian's fault, and suddenly a dozen men were below to fetch him. Allende did not stop them; he could do naught but stand, and wait.

And still the monster did nothing.

Finally Allende gathered his courage in his hands. He was the captain, and he was old. Better that he face the beast than consign any of the men, much less a passenger Venetian. He spoke in his loudest voice, "Who are you, fell Mer-maid? What do you want from us poor sailors?"

The monster tilted her head and moved forward, over the ship. An overwhelming smell of rotted fish extended with her breath. Sailors fainted.

"Come back to me, Marcello," the monster said, craning her neck to look back to the rear of the boat. Grown men trembled.

Allende looked back. There was the Venetian, the small man in ragged noble-clothes who'd prayed the entirety of his stay aboard the ship. A dozen of his sailors hoisted him forward.

"Marcello," the monster said, her voice rumbling like the fires of God.

The men holding the Venetian dropped him and ran, trembling, as far from the monster as could be.

The Venetian brushed himself off and stood. His anger was apparent in his visage, and he carried not a whiff of fear. "Mother, what are you doing so far south?" he called out. "I told you I would not stay."

The monster drew back, offended, and the sailors trembled. She frowned in a horrific way down at the Venetian. "Your father treats with the French crusaders, and I grew bored," she said. "Have done with your silly rebellion, I beg of you. We will visit the undersea palaces. I will make you your favorite boiled squid."

"I told you when I left, Mother. This—"

de Tera finally found his voice and interrupted. "Monster! How dare you interfere in the lives of men! I told you, Captain, the—"

"Quiet," the monster said, in a voice that shook the entirety of the ship. "Your betters are talking."

"My betters!" de Tera turned so red with rage, Allende was certain he would collapse. But the man gestured with a fist, distain and rage carrying him away. "I get my authority from His Majesty and His Holiness directly! There are none my better here, much less a disgusting, ugly creature as does not know how to be quiet as suits a proper woman!"

Now the monster turned to him directly. She reared up to a magnificent height, her unbound breasts coming out of the water. "What did you say to me?" she said, in a voice most terrible.

"I... I..." de Tera stammered, suddenly afraid. He babbled on for a moment, some incomprehensible thing about His Holiness the Pope and the wrath of His Majesty, while the thick, inky sea curled up a ribbon of water, up and up the side of the ship.

Allende swallowed bile. "Dear Mer-Maid, pray have mercy on our ship. We mean no harm..."

de Tera continued his tirade, his rage overcoming fear until he screamed at the monster. The monster looked back, its teeth shown fiercely.

The ribbon kept coming, up and up by slow degrees, its thick darkness terrifying as it stood against all reason, against all rule of natural law. It curled then, into a noose—and darted, like a fish, to collapse around de Tera's throat.

de Tera flew overboard. He hit the surface of the sea with a bone-shattering thwap, screamed like a tortured animal, and then was sucked slowly under its viscous surface until he was seen no more.

Allende held back bile. Others, sailors, screamed and vomited most foully.

"Anyone else want to interfere in my conversation with my son?" the monster asked, all too quietly, into the silence.

Again, Allende must speak when no one else could. He opened his mouth, but a small sound came out, a sound unfitting for a captain. He gripped his hands so firmly his nails drew blood. He would speak. For the lives of his men and his own immortal soul, he would speak.

But the Venetian had walked forward until he had passed him, close, far too close to the monster that would surely destroy the ship at any moment.

"I will make my way in the world," the Venetian told the monster very intensely. "I have said it many times, and many times you have not heard. So long as I am in Venice, I am the doge's son, I am your son. All are silenced long before I prove my mettle. How then shall I ever know what I am truly made of? How then shall I know who I really am? You hold me back from your fears, mother, you make me small."

The monster settled down again into the thickness of the sea. "But what am I to do? I am lonely," she complained quietly, with a deep emotion. "Can I not come with you on your adventure? I will be a great help in danger."

The Venetian shook his head, his fists held tightly against his body, and Allende knew he would defy the monster. What matter of foul lineage the man claimed, their fighting would tear the ship into small pieces and Allende's crew would not survive. His last voyage would end in shame.

And so he must speak, with whatever honeyed words he'd ever learned in purchasing goods from difficult foreign men. "My lady, I regret," He began slowly, that noose of water always before him. "I regret, my lady, you cannot join us. Your magnificence is too large to fit in our small ship. Pray, only--"

She cut him off. "I can become smaller," she said, in the tone of a fell child overcoming objections to her will.

In a blink, she was gone, and in her place a beautiful woman of average height stood on deck, fully clothed in a gown of vermillion satin and lace in the latest fashion. "I have not quite so much power in this form, but for traveling it will do," she said. "I will be a great help to you, I swear it by all that is holy, Marcello."

"I will tolerate your foolishness any more. Leave me be or I will do far worse than father," Marcello said, in a tone so terrible Allende feared for his ship and his very life. If such magic lived in the monster, that she could become small, what magic lay in the small man who'd inhabited the Josephina?

"My lady," Allende forced out again, through choked throat.

She moved until she was very nearly on top of him, inches from his face. "Why you are a handsome fellow."

He shook, but he stood his ground. He was drawn to her, a strange pull that must be magic, as she looked him over.

Her porcelain skin seemed nearly translucent, her eyes large and rimmed with thick lashes, her nose small and perfect. Her thick dark hair was braided with pearls, her dress rich and beautiful. She was the picture of the noblewoman he'd dreamed of, in his quiet moments, the prize he had never sold enough goods to merit. But under the skin she was no quiet widow, no blushing gentlewoman. She met his gaze boldly, and her powers could crush him in a moment, he feared. That inky sea was her true soul and he must not be enraptured by the appearance of things.

The Venetian sighed. "Mother, leave off tormenting the captain. I will not go with you, and you cannot stay, no matter what treaty you have made with the local seagod. You know very well that the sea will not lose its viscous ink so long as you stand here. It is a poor adventure indeed when one never moves. Go back home, I will be back in a year or two if things go well. I have promised you thrice already."

She turned, and stamped her foot at her son. "It isn't fair! You get all the fun while your father talks to tedious men and cavorts with silly mistresses! I will not be ignored." The sea grew shaky below them, until the ship's boards groaned with the strain of this unexpected movement.

"And I will not adventure with you any longer. You must go alone." The Venetian's tone was quiet, sure, full of his own power. The air seemed tense around him, tense so much that Allende once more knew a battle between them would crush them all.

"Adventuring alone is not what I want."

A sailor fainted just in Allende's periphery, and the ship groaned as the inky water began to rise. Shortly they would all be like de Tera, lost at sea, swallowed up against all nature. de Tera had been right, it seemed, about the Venetian. He was a magician, surely, if not worse. This one fare would kill all of his crew, and Allende was responsible for all of their lives.

"Give me your word you shall not harm the ship, my crew, or myself in any way," he heard himself saying.

"What?" the Venetian asked. The woman-creature turned as well.

"You, lady. If I go with you, give me your word you will leave my ship be forever after and that you will not harm me."

"Of what benefit is that to me?" the woman-creature said.

She was petulant, perhaps, but there was a mind there to appeal to. He prayed that there was. And great beauty, beauty such as he had never seen. This was to be his last journey, after all, and he could at least save the sailors from their fate.

"My lady, you clearly travel by means other than ships," he said cautiously. "You have offered to take your son to underwater palaces, and unless he be far different than any other man, you have means to keep him hale. I have spent forty years at sea. I have traveled near all of the world, and what I have not, I have studied. If you give me your word to leave my ship be, not to harm me nor to allow me to come to harm in any way, I will go with you and show you all that I have seen. You wish to adventure, and to not adventure alone. I will go with you."

She frowned, but he could see her interest. "I know the sea better than any man."

He gripped his courage in his hands and stepped toward her. "Do you know the land? The bazaars of Istanbul. The camels of Arabia. The spice markets of the Indies, and the silk spinners of the Orient. Creatures with long noses that princes ride upon to war. Trees so large a dozen men holding hands cannot measure their breadth. There are wonders out there, and adventures a plenty. Who is to say your son should be the only one to test his mettle against the wide world?"

"This is a terrible idea," the Venetian said. "She will break you like a shell the first time she has a temper."

"I will not," the woman-creature said. "I rather like the captain. And if he offers me adventure..."

Allende stopped. What had he promised? What had he gotten himself into? "Adventure indeed I will offer you, if..." Allende said.

She took a breath, and truly considered. Allende nearly reconsidered, but the ship groaned loudly as the pressure of the seas built. Sailors whimpered, and he knew he had no choice.

The woman-creature smiled, a smile that lit up the sea. "Very well. I promise to leave your ship and your crew unharmed. I promise not to harm you, nor to allow you to come to harm to whatever degree I have influence. I will not be held an oathbreaker if you court danger without my presence," she added. There was wit there, and compassion, which sat oddly with the petulance and beauty. Perhaps she might deal fairly, if she found what she sought. He prayed she would, for upon such things his life depended.

"Thank you, my lady," he added, through his real fear. But beside it, perhaps a small excitement, perhaps a knowledge that this, after all, would not be his last adventure, his last voyage at sea. "I pray thee, give me a scant hour to settle my ship for my absence and to gather things." He took a breath and considered. "Am I able to bring a sea trunk?" His life—for as long as it lasted in her presence—would be much improved by the taking of supplies.

She considered. "Perhaps a large sack, something you can carry about your person. We shall have plenty of fish to feed upon, but the sea does get cold at times. Go, and I will talk with my son."

"Very well, my lady," Allende said, regret and excitement mixing within his gut.

"How will father feel about this?" the Venetian asked in a stern tone. "Consider it, mother. With both of us gone, who will take care of him? Pray, reconsider."

"He should take care of himself, or find yet another mistress to do so," the woman-creature said. "I will have an adventure."

The two moved up to the helm, and continued to talk in low tones. Allende stopped to speak with Ortiz, his first mate, currently huddled behind the mast, to give him courage and brace him for the responsibilities to come—if they lived.

After, he gripped his fate in his hands and passed belowdecks, passing common sailor upon sailor who cowered away from him, as if he were contaminated. The ship creaked again, more urgently, with the edge of the sound of snapping wood.

He had pledged his life to the survival of the ship and its crew, year after year. If he were to keep the pledge, he must move far faster than the hour.

But if the beauty and the wit of the woman-creature held, he would have one more great adventure, and live on the seas and in the foreign lands some time longer. Or he would die, as he had lived, a part of the sea and all its wonders after all. Now to assemble supplies and to determine where to take her first, and how to navigate with only the stars, a sextant, and the inky black sea.

Thank you for reading.
Readers like you make
everything possible.

Find out more about me and my work and read excerpts, short stories, deleted scenes and more at http://www.ahugheswriter.com. There's also a contact form there to get in touch with me. I love hearing from readers!

While you're there, consider signing up for the newsletter for updates on new releases and the occasional free short story here: http://www.ahugheswriter.com/email-signup.

Want to spread the love even more? Consider leaving a review where you bought this book. Reviews help other readers find stories they love and help the series grow.

Thank you again for reading!

Want more work by Alex? Check out:

*The Mindspace Investigations Series:

    Rabbit Trick (short story)
    Clean
    Payoff (novella)
    Sharp
    Marked
    Vacant
    Fluid (novella)

*Other Works:

    The Three Words Project:
    Short Stories Inspired by Readers

    How to Drive Yourself Crazy
    as a Writer: A Satire

About the Author

Alex Hughes, the author of the award-winning Mindspace Investigations series from Roc, has lived in the Atlanta area since the age of eight. She is a graduate of the prestigious Odyssey Writing Workshop, and her short fiction has been published in several markets including *EveryDay Fiction, Thunder on the Battlefield* and *White Cat Magazine.* She is an avid cook and foodie, a trivia buff, and a science geek, and loves to talk about neuroscience, the Food Network, and writing craft—but not necessarily all at the same time. You can visit her at Twitter at @ahugheswriter or on the web at www. ahugheswriter.com.

21294000R00038

Printed in Great Britain
by Amazon